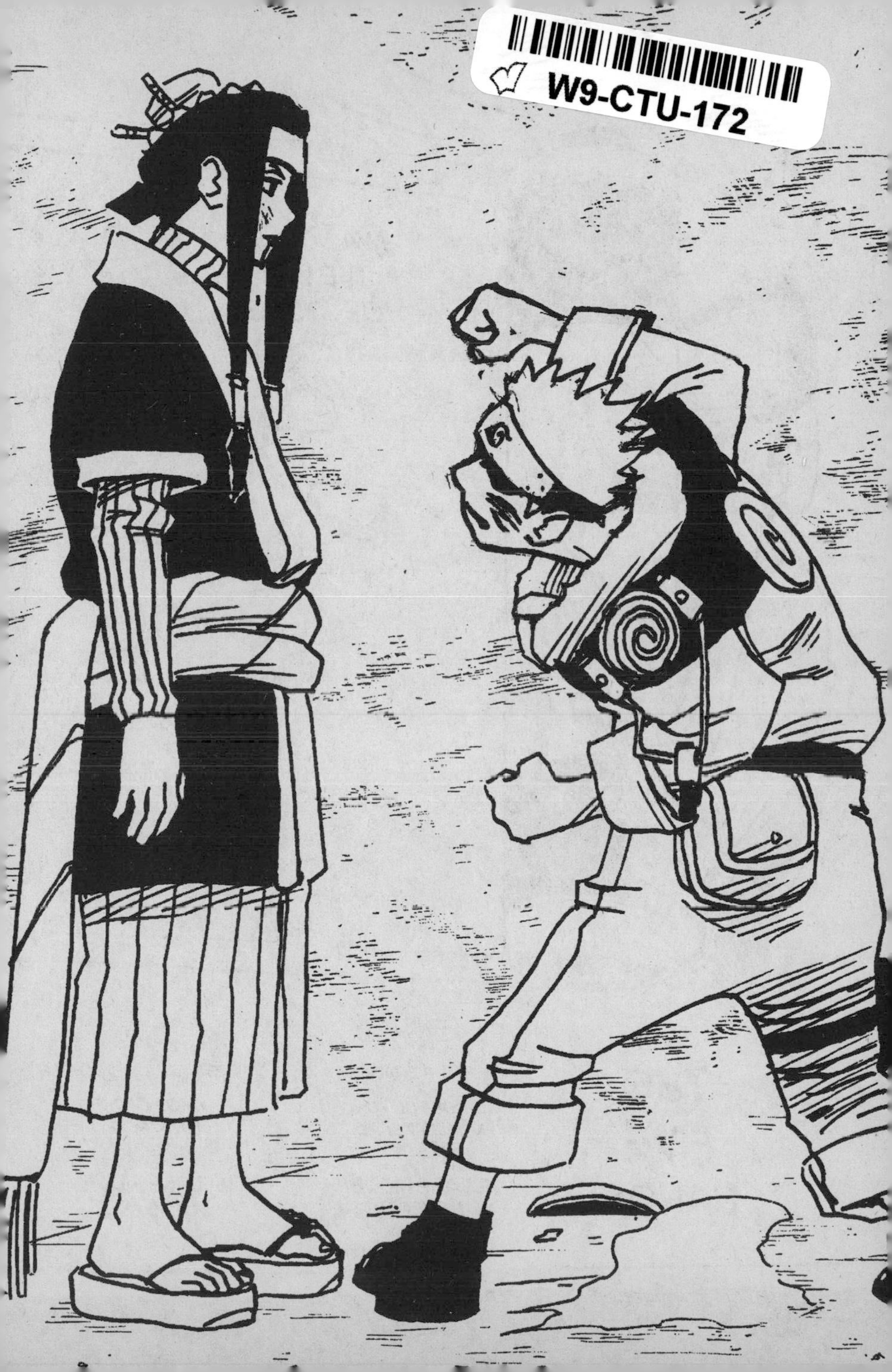

IWA NO KUNI:
THE LAND
OF STONES

SUNA NO KUNI:
THE LAND
OF SAND

THE
FIVE
LANDS

THE FIRE SHADOW

KONOHA NO KUNI
KONOHARGURE
NO SATO:

**VILLAGE HIDDEN
IN THE LEAVES**

THE WATER SHADOW

KIRO NO KUNI
KIRIGAKURE
NO SATO:

**VILLAGE HIDDEN
IN THE MIST**

KUMO NO KUNI:
THE LAND OF
THE CLOUDS

KIRO NO KUNI:
THE LAND OF
MIST AND FOG

KONOHA NO KUNI:
THE LAND OF
TREE AND LEAF

THE LIGHTNING SHADOW

KUMO NO KUNI
KUMOGAKURE
NO SATO:

**VILLAGE HIDDEN
IN THE CLOUDS**

THE WIND SHADOW

SUNA NO KUNI
SUNAGAKURE
NO SATO:

**VILLAGE HIDDEN
IN THE SAND**

THE EARTH SHADOW

IWA NO KUNI
IWAGAKURE
NO SATO:

**VILLAGE HIDDEN
IN THE SHADOW**

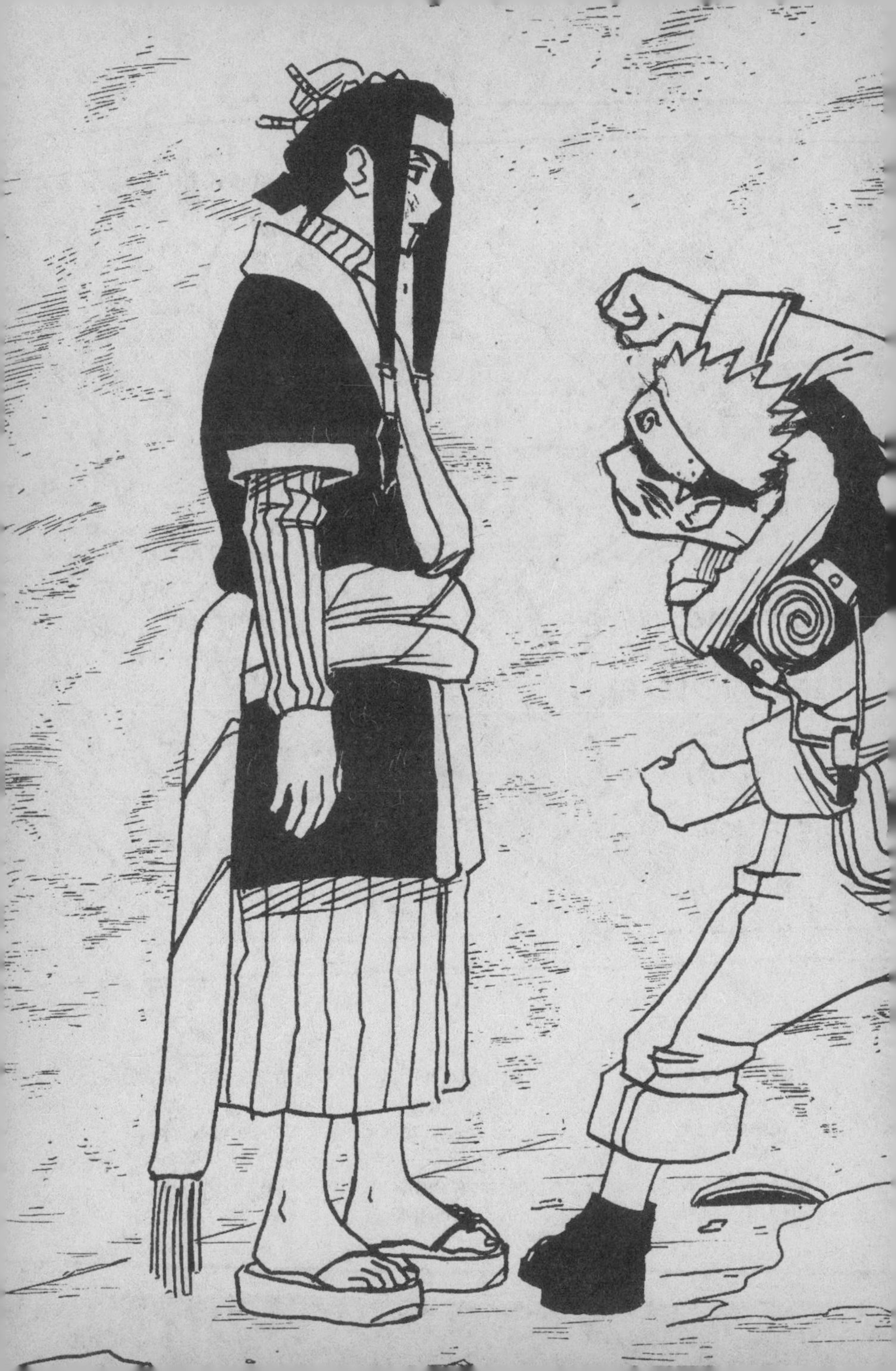

NARUTO

THE NEXT LEVEL

ORIGINAL STORY BY **MASASHI KISHIMOTO**

ADAPTED BY TRACEY WEST

vizkids

VIZ MEDIA

SAN FRANCISCO

NARUTO THE NEXT LEVEL
CHAPTER BOOK 7

Illustrations: Masashi Kishimoto
Design: Courtney Utt

Published by VIZ Media, LLC
P.O. Box 77010
San Francisco, CA 94107

www.viz.com

West, Tracey, 1965-
Naruto: the next level /original story by Masashi Kishimoto; adapted by Tracey West;
[illustrations, Masashi Kishimoto].
    p. cm. -- (Naruto; 7)
"A VIZ Kids Book."
Summary: As the battle over the bridge heightens, Naruto and his friends learn what it means to
truly become a ninja--sometimes you have to fight to win--then deal with the consequences.
ISBN-13: 978-1-4215-2317-0
ISBN-10: 1-4215-2317-5
[1. Ninja--Fiction. 2. Japan--Fiction] I. Kishimoto, Masashi, 1974- II. Title.
PZ7.W51937Nar 2009
[Fic]--dc22
    2008037691

Printed in the U.S.A.
First printing, May 2009

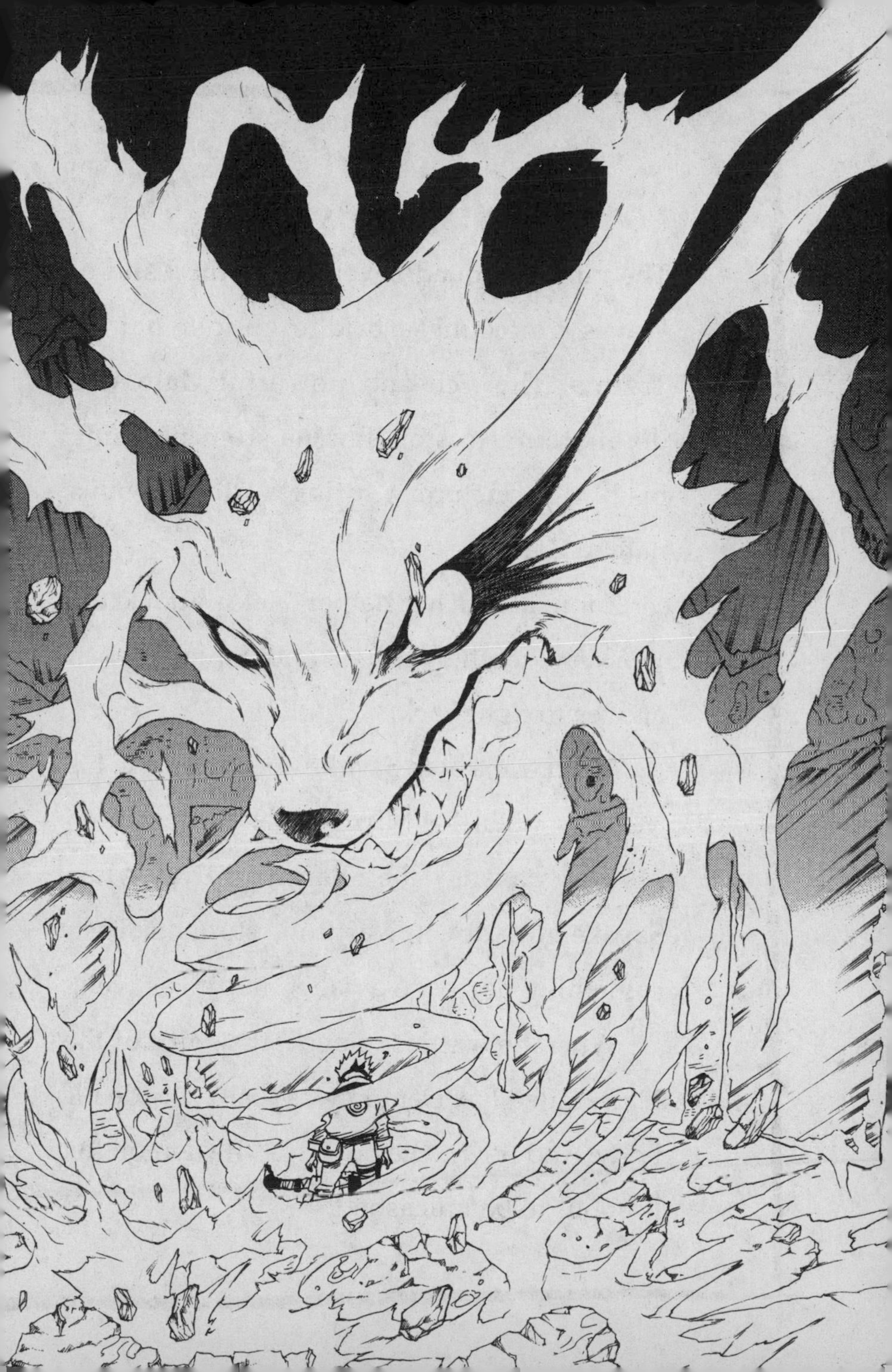

THE STORY SO FAR

The ninja of Squad Seven are in the Land of Waves protecting a bridge builder named Tazuna. The rich and powerful Gato will do anything to stop Tazuna from finishing his bridge, including hiring a ruthless ninja named Zabuza.

Zabuza and his helper Haku attack the workers on the bridge, and Squad Seven arrives to fight back.

Haku traps both Sasuke and Naruto in his Magic Crystal Ice Mirrors. Sasuke's hidden power awakens—the Sharingan Eye! When Sasuke goes down, Naruto is stunned. Then something begins to awaken in him as well.

When he was just a baby, the spirit of the Nine-Tailed Fox Demon was sealed inside his body. And now...the power of the demon fox is about to be unleashed!

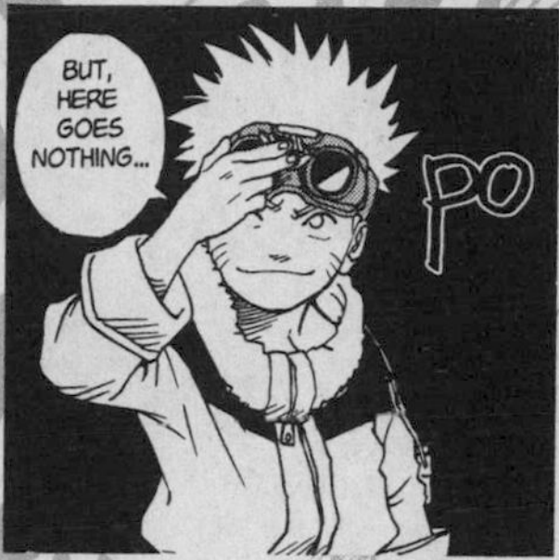
BUT, HERE GOES NOTHING...
PO

Naruto
ナルト

Naruto is training to be a ninja. He's a bit of a clown. But deep down, he's serious about becoming the world's greatest shinobi!

Sakura
春野サクラ

Naruto and Sasuke's classmate. She has a crush on Sasuke, who ignores her. In return, she picks on Naruto, who has a crush on *her*.

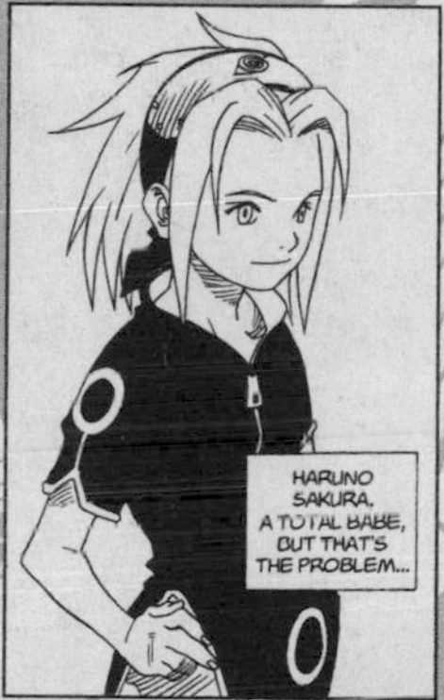
HARUNO SAKURA. A TOTAL BABE, BUT THAT'S THE PROBLEM...

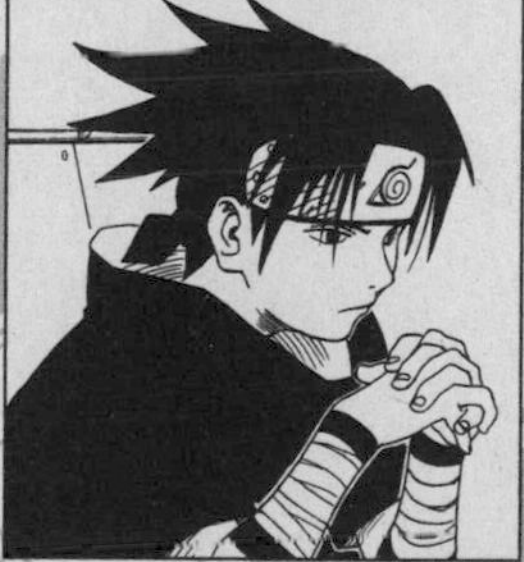

Sasuke
うちはサスケ

The top student in Naruto's class and a member of the prestigious Uchiha clan.

A CHILLY mist covered a bridge that jutted out from the Land of Waves.

A warrior named Zabuza hid in the mist. He had traveled to this land to stop the bridge from being built. A small group of young ninja wanted to stop him.

He wasn't about to let them.

Kakashi, the experienced ninja leader of Squad Seven, silently tracked Zabuza.

Sakura, the only girl ninja in the squad, guarded old Mr. Tazuna, the bridge builder.

The mist now covered a prison created by Zabuza's ninja helper, Haku. The prison's walls were large mirrors made of ice. Inside, Sasuke lay on the ground, as still as a stone. Naruto was filled with rage. He looked over at Haku, his eyes burning like coals. Haku stood inside one of the mirrors, his face hidden behind a white mask.

"I WILL STOP YOU!" Naruto yelled.

Fiery red flames rose up around Naruto and Sasuke. The flames whirled around them like a blazing tornado. Then they lashed out, striking at the ice mirrors. The ice shattered. Sharp shards fell down like rain.

What chakra is this? Haku wondered.

The flames rose higher and higher into the air. They began to take shape, forming the head of a snarling beast with glowing eyes and sharp teeth.

Haku watched Naruto in awe. Both Haku and Naruto were only about thirteen years old. But Naruto trained under Kakashi. Haku was Zabuza's loyal follower. It was Haku's duty to take down the ninja who wanted to stop his master.

Impossible! I can see the boy's chakra, Haku realized. *It's scary!*

Naruto began to snarl like a wild animal. The cuts on his arms where Haku's needles had found their mark quickly faded. His fists curled up and long, sharp claws grew from his fingertips.

His wounds are healing themselves! Haku thought. *Who—or what—on earth is he?*

Naruto raised his head and glared at Haku. Haku gasped. Naruto's eyes were dark red!

Out in the mist, Kakashi felt Naruto's chakra energy.

Is this Zabuza's doing? Kakashi wondered. *No! This energy is evil—but I've felt it before...*

Zabuza sensed the energy too. *Something about this chakra fills me with dread*, he thought. *Kakashi? No, it's too big for Kakashi. Then whose is it?*

Naruto! Kakashi realized. *It can't be, after all this time! Is the binding spell over? Has the seal broken?* He concentrated for a moment.

We're safe for now, he thought. *The seal is cracked a little but not broken. The power of the Nine-Tailed Fox is coming through.*

Kakashi moved quickly. He untied a small tube attached to the front of his vest. He flipped it open to reveal a long, thin scroll of paper inside. Writing in black ink covered the paper.

"Listen to me, Zabuza," Kakashi called into the mist. "I'm a busy man, you're a busy man. So what do you say we stop fooling around?"

Kakashi looked at the writing on the scroll. Then he rolled it back into the tube. He gripped the scroll with his thumbs and put his palms together. His middle and index fingers were extended in front of his face. He was ready to make his move.

"Let's wrap this thing up right *NOW*," he challenged. "One big move. Winner takes all."

Zabuza's voice came through the mist. "I'm interested," he said. "So what's left? Show me what you've got."

Back inside the prison of mirrors, Naruto charged at Haku. He ran on all fours like an animal, growling.

Haku quickly aimed an attack of sharp needles right at Naruto. They sliced through the air.

"*Aaaaaaar!*" Naruto let out a roar. The flames of chakra energy swirled around him, sending the needles flying away.

Haku couldn't believe it. *He deflected them… without even touching them!*

Naruto kept charging, crashing into the mirror with incredible force. The glass broke. Haku jumped out, and Naruto fell backward.

He skidded to a stop on the icy floor.

Haku knew his speed would protect him from Naruto's power.

I've got to make it to the next mirror!

HAKU RACED to the next mirror so fast that he could barely be seen by the human eye.

But Naruto was faster.

BAM!

Naruto smacked into Haku, who fell down.

Haku was shocked. *He couldn't have!*

Naruto pawed the floor with his feet. The chakra flames were sharp as knives now, tearing the mirrors to pieces. The icy prison began to crumble. The whole place had been created with Haku's power. Without that power, it all would fall. Haku pressed his fingers together, trying to keep his ninjutsu from being destroyed.

This is bad, Haku thought, as he strained to hold on to his energy. *I can't fight back against this chakra anymore!*

Naruto reached out and gripped Haku's wrist with his left hand. He curled his right hand into a fist.

POW!

The super strong punch slammed into Haku's mask. Haku flew back, breaking through the wall of ice. His body skidded along the ground. Naruto chased after him.

Panting, Naruto watched Haku slowly stand up. The white mask was cracked.

"Master Zabuza," Haku said softly.

The pieces of the mask fell to the ground, one by one. Naruto raced toward Haku, his fist clenched and ready for another attack.

Then he saw Haku's face. His dark eyes looked sad.

"I...am finished," Haku said.

Naruto stopped. The beast inside him wanted to attack. But Naruto held back.

He knew that face.

"You're the kid I met this morning," Naruto said.

Haku had found Naruto sleeping in the woods after a night of training. The two of them had talked. That Haku was nice— nothing like the fierce ninja who had hurt Sasuke.

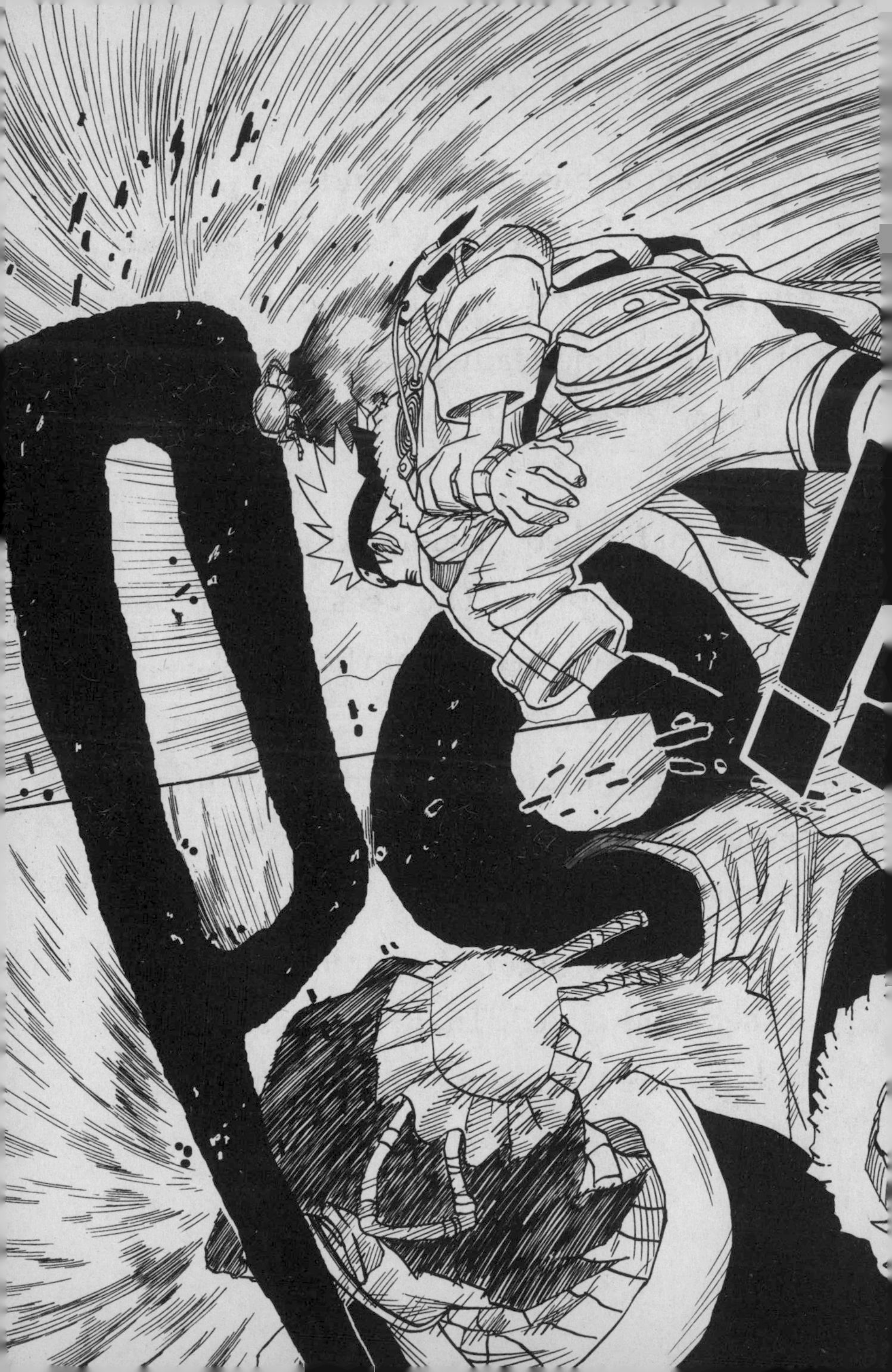

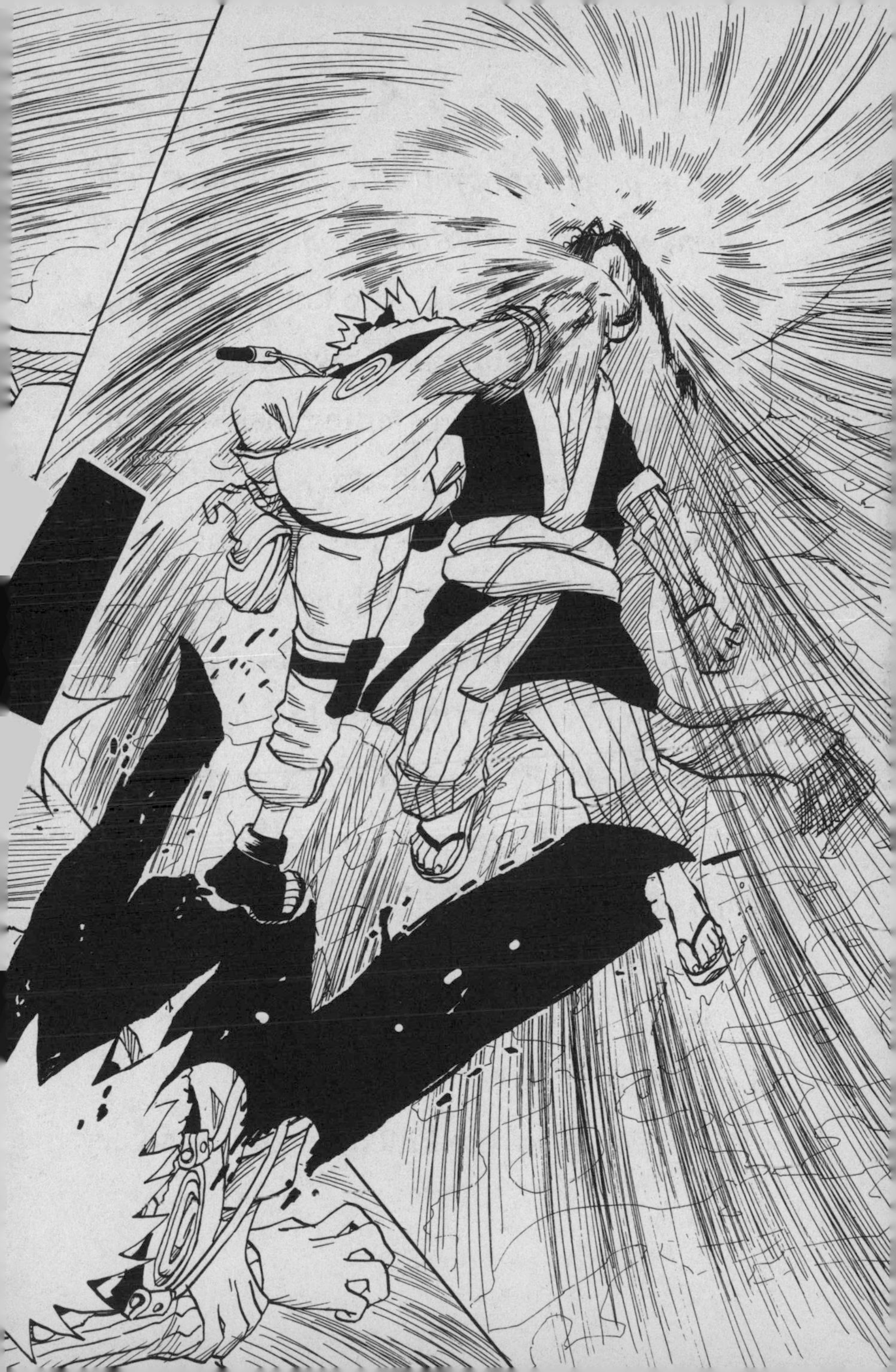

When people are protecting someone special to them, only then can they become truly strong, Haku had said. Now Naruto knew that Haku was protecting Zabuza. But why?

The beast was slowly fading inside Naruto now. He listened as Haku spoke.

"Some people believe that showing mercy to an enemy is kind," Haku went on. "But they are wrong. It is worse to be kept alive when you have **NOTHING** to live for."

"**SAY WHAT?**" Naruto asked.

"Master Zabuza has no use for a weak ninja," Haku replied. "I can no longer serve him. My dream is over."

"Why?" Naruto cried. "Why do you care about that creep?"

"My parents were killed when I was very

young," Haku replied. "I was born in a snowy village in the Land of Mist. Our land was at war for many years. Ninja with kekkei genkai like me were hated and feared."

"**KEKKEI GENKAI?**" Naruto asked.

"It is a name for a ninja skill that is passed down through members of a clan," Haku explained. "A skill like mine, that allows me to turn water into ice."

Naruto nodded. He knew about those special ninjutsu. His teacher, Kakashi, had a kekkei genkai—his powerful Sharingan Eye.

"After the wars, ninja with kekkei genkai

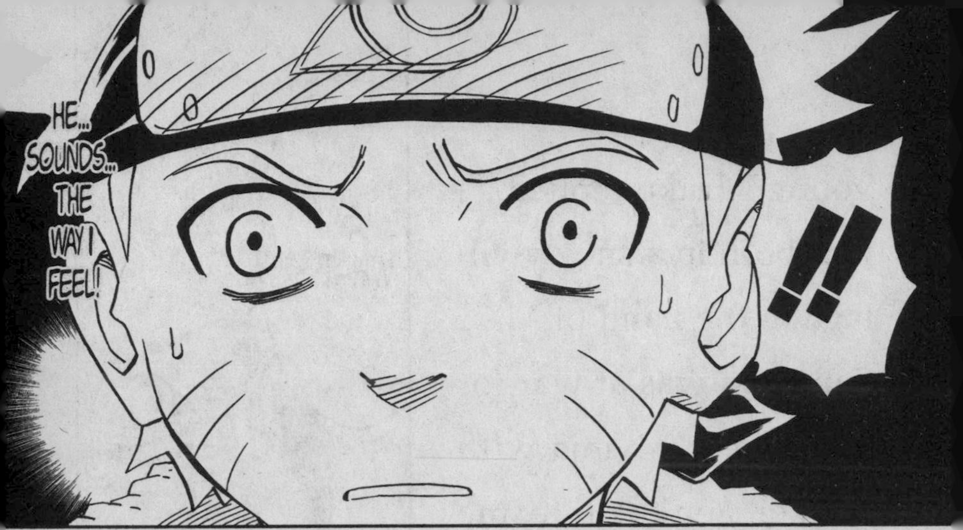
HE... SOUNDS... THE WAY I FEEL!
!!

were hunted down. I was lucky to escape with my life. But I was alone in the world. Unwanted. Shunned."

Naruto's blue eyes widened. *I know how he feels*. The adults in Naruto's village knew about the fox monster inside him. They had treated him like an outcast ever since he was a baby.

"Master Zabuza found me and adopted me," Haku said. "He didn't hate me because of the kekkei genkai. He wanted that power.

He needed it."

A tear flowed down Haku's cheek. "I was so happy."

Haku looked at Naruto.

"Didn't you tell me this morning that you wanted to become the number one ninja in your village? That you wanted everyone to respect you?" Haku asked. "If you had someone in your life who wasn't afraid of you when everyone else was, wouldn't that person become the most important person in your life?"

Naruto thought of his teacher, Master Iruka. He was the first person to ever treat Naruto with kindness. Naruto

would never, ever forget that.

"Forgive me, Master Zabuza," Haku said softly. "I have failed you."

FURTHER DOWN the bridge, Kakashi prepared to face Zabuza. He made a series of hand signs. Then he pressed his right palm to the ground and covered it with his left palm.

ONNNNNNNNNNNNG!

The air crackled with the energy of the powerful ninjutsu.

"Earth Style!" Kakashi yelled. "Fanged Vengeance Technique!"

"This will get you nowhere, Kakashi!" Zabuza shouted through the mist. "You can't even tell where I truly am! But I know exactly where you are and how to defeat you. You are trapped in my spell."

Zabuza lifted two fingers in front of his face. But before he could perform his ninjutsu, he felt the bridge beneath his feet begin to break apart.

What now? Zabuza wondered.

The concrete beneath his feet exploded. A pack of snarling dogs burst through the bridge, snapping at his legs.

"No!" Zabuza cried.

The dogs sprang at him from all sides. They were strong, muscular beasts wearing ninja vests. They chomped onto Zabuza's arms and legs. The largest was a huge bulldog who wore a spiked collar around his

neck. The bulldog clamped onto his shoulder, holding him down.

As Zabuza's power faded, the mist began to disappear.

"When your eyes and ears have let you down, you can always follow your **NOSE**," Kakashi said. "This summoning is used for tracking—with the sense of smell."

He stepped toward Zabuza.

"That's why I let you hurt me earlier," Kakashi explained. "The smell of my blood is on your sword. My little ninja pups couldn't miss it. Every dog has his nose, and they all know you stink. Who is trapped in whose spell now?"

Zabuza grunted. The dogs had him pinned to the spot. He couldn't move.

Kakashi pulled down the mask on his face, revealing his left eye: the Sharingan Eye. Strange black symbols swirled around the red iris of his eye.

"The fog is lifting. I can see your future," Kakashi said. *"It's not good."*

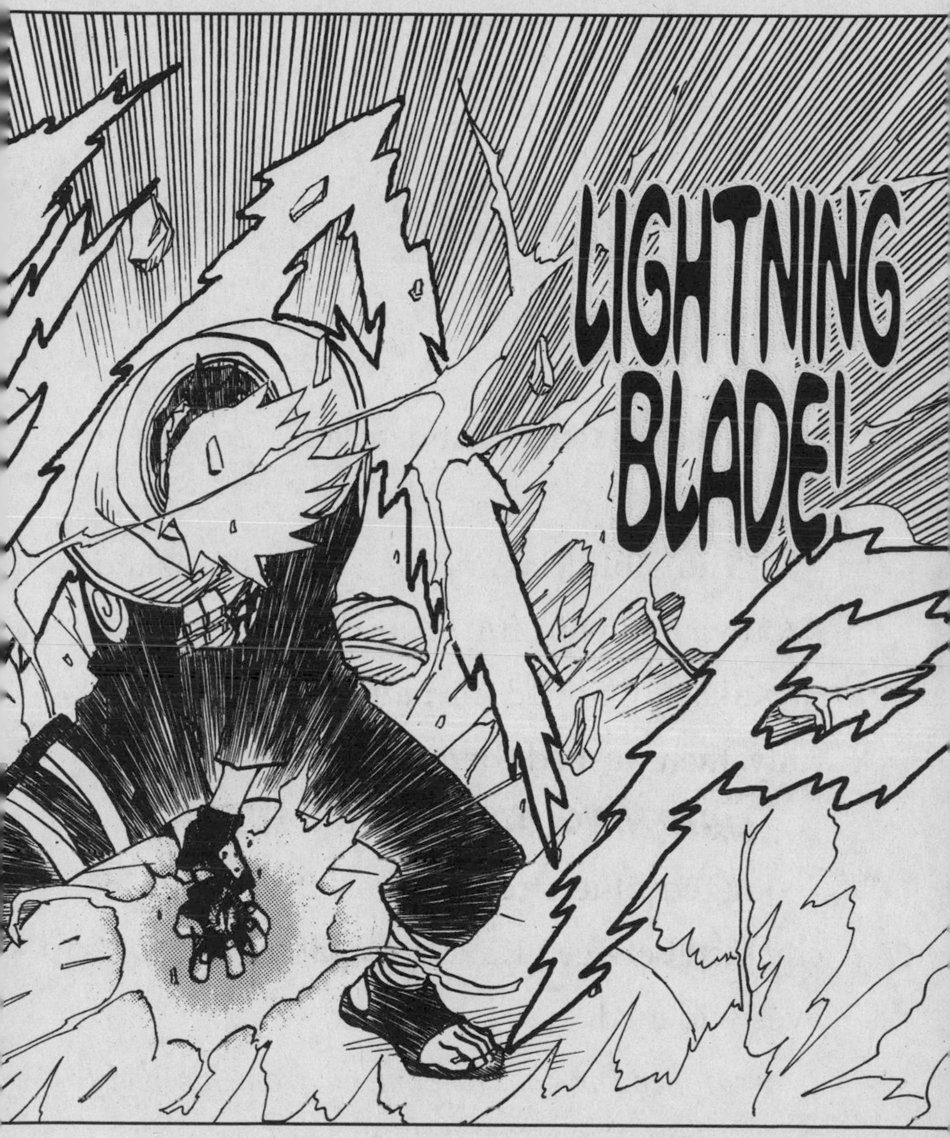
LIGHTNING BLADE!

"QUIT BLUFFING," Zabuza said. "So far you are all talk."

"Who's bluffing now?" Kakashi asked. "You've had your fun, Zabuza."

Kakashi slapped his palms together forcefully, then pushed them toward the ground.

"*LIGHTNING BLADE!*" Kakashi cried.

Jagged blue streaks of electric lightning crackled between Kakashi's palms. Zabuza's eyes widened.

I can see the chakra coming from his body.

Zabuza knew that only very powerful chakra could be seen with the eye.

"You're too dangerous," Kakashi went on. As he spoke, the energy grew stronger and brighter between his hands. "Mr. Tazuna, the man you're trying to kill, is the heart and spirit of this place. The bridge he is trying to build is the land's only *HOPE*. You are willing to destroy everything here just to get what you want. That is not what a true ninja does."

"Spare me the lesson," Zabuza sneered. "I'm fighting for my own ideals. And I'm not about to stop."

"Give up now," Kakashi replied calmly.

Back on the other part of the bridge, Naruto's voice grew quiet. "If we met some other way, in some other place, you and I would probably have been friends," he said to Haku.

Naruto gripped the kunai that was strapped to his right leg. Minutes ago Naruto had wanted to hurt Haku for what he did to Sasuke. But it didn't feel right now.

But then a shudder went through Haku's body. The lost, sad look left his face. He seemed to be filled with new energy.

"I'm sorry, Naruto," Haku said. He quickly made a hand sign. "**YOU CAN'T STOP ME YET**."

And then he vanished, leaving only a puddle of water behind him.

"Huh?" Naruto turned to see that the mist had mostly evaporated.

Elsewhere, Kakashi was charging at Zabuza. Big dogs had Zabuza pinned down so he couldn't move. Streaks of lightning flew from Kakashi's hands. Naruto gasped. That was one powerful ninjutsu!

Then Kakashi struck, hurling the lightning at Zabuza with his right hand. Zabuza braced himself for the attack. And then...

Haku teleported in front of Zabuza.

Kakashi couldn't stop in time. He slammed into Haku with the entire force of the lightning attack. The dogs gripping Zabuza vanished one by one.

Suddenly there was an explosion of light and smoke. When the light faded, Haku fell forward against Kakashi's body.

"Zabuza…Sir…" Haku said in a cracked voice. Then he closed his eyes and was still.

"Heh, heh," Zabuza laughed. "You said my future didn't look good. But you were wrong again, Kakashi."

ALL OF the houses in the Land of Waves overlooked the ocean. Docks built with wood planks connected rows of homes separated by water. Long ago the houses had been painted in bright colors—yellows, blues, pinks, and greens. But after years of hard times in the land the paint was faded and cracked.

A young boy ran along the docks. He had wide dark eyes, and dark hair peeked out from under the white and blue striped cap on his head. His name was Inari and he was the grandson of Tazuna, the bridge builder.

Inari stopped in front of one of the homes and banged on the door.

"Mister Giichi, open up please!" he yelled. "I need you to come with me to the bridge. If we stick together, we can beat Gato and his whole gang!"

Inari paused, thinking of his father. His dad had been the only person in the village brave enough to stand up to the evil Gato. And Gato's men had killed Inari's father.

Inari had lived in fear after that. Then

Naruto and Squad Seven had come to his home to protect his grandfather. They weren't afraid of Gato.

And now Inari wasn't afraid either.

The man replied from behind his locked door. "I'm sorry, Inari, we're not going to fight back anymore," he said. "Your father was a hero. But he's gone now. We don't want any more losses. No regrets."

"I don't want to have regrets either," Inari replied. "That's why I have to fight. I love my mom, my grandpa, and everyone in this village. And I understand now that I can't protect anyone by being a big crybaby."

Inari turned and left.

Inari's mother, Tsunami, didn't like the idea of Inari going by himself.

"You can't go to the bridge alone!" Tsunami cried.

"Have to. Nobody will go with me," Inari told her. He sat on a bench in the kitchen, strapping on his sandals. He had traded his hat for a helmet made from a cooking pot and string. On the bench next to him was a crossbow he had made out of some scrap wood. A quiver of homemade arrows was strapped to his back.

"But you're just a little boy!" Tsunami pleaded.

"But I know how to fight," Inari said. He walked to the door, stopped, and grinned at his mom. "'Cause I'm my daddy's son."

He opened the door and stepped outside. What he saw there made him stop and gasp in shock.

6

NARUTO RAN over to Haku who was now lying on the ground. Naruto knew nobody could have survived such a powerful attack.

"What?" he couldn't say anything more.

Across the bridge, Sakura and Tazuna looked shocked.

"Isn't that the boy in the mask?" Tazuna asked.

"He jumped between us to save Zabuza," said Kakashi.

Zabuza laughed again. "Heh. That was

brilliant, Haku." He reached for the huge sword strapped to his back.

Kakashi realized that Zabuza planned to attack him.

"Master Kakashi!" Sakura yelled in warning.

Zabuza swung the sword above his head. "I really did find a treasure in that gutter," he gloated. "To think he gave me this chance to finally finish you off, Kakashi!"

Kakashi held Haku close to him and swiftly somersaulted backward, landing far from the reach of Zabuza's sword. Then he gently laid Haku on the bridge.

Naruto glared at Zabuza, his eyes blazing with fury. "You rotten creep!" he yelled.

"Naruto, stay out of this," Kakashi called

out. **"This is my fight."**

Sakura brightened. "Naruto? Naruto, you're still alive!" she called out happily.

"Sakura," Naruto said. He was relieved to see her too.

"So what about Sasuke?" Sakura asked. "Where is he?"

Naruto flinched. Hearing Sasuke's name was like feeling a sword through his body.

He tried to answer Sakura—but all he could do was try not to cry.

Sakura's face went pale. Naruto was alive. But Sasuke...

"*FOCUS, KAKASHI!*" Zabuza taunted. "Don't let yourself be distracted!"

He charged across the bridge at Kakashi. Kakashi pushed him away with one strong kick. Zabuza went flying backward.

Tazuna looked down at Sakura. "I'll stay with you, so you won't be disobeying your master's order to protect me."

Sakura nodded, and Tazuna took her hand. They walked past Naruto. He couldn't even bear to look at them.

They stopped at Sasuke who was lying still on the ground.

Sakura's eyes filled with tears.

NARUTO CLOSED his eyes as the sound of Sakura crying carried over the bridge. He clenched his hand over his chest, trying to keep his emotions inside.

Behind Naruto, Zabuza got to his feet. Kakashi's kick had taken him by surprise.

Why can't I keep up? Zabuza wondered.

He raised his giant sword.

"AAAAAAAAH!" He roared as he charged down the bridge toward Kakashi.

48

Kakashi simply held out his right hand. Zabuza slammed into it, and the force sent him hurling backward. He quickly jumped back to his feet and attacked again.

But Kakashi was no longer in front of him. The ninja had jumped as fast as lightning and now stood behind Zabuza. He tightly gripped the back of Zabuza's neck.

"There's no way you can beat me," Kakashi said calmly. "It's over. You just don't know it yet."

With one swift move, Kakashi delivered a blow to Zabuza's left arm. It dangled limply.

"*This is goodbye*, Demon," Kakashi promised.

Zabuza spun around, trying to attack, but Kakashi was too fast. He struck Zabuza's right arm with another blow.

"Now you can't use either arm," Kakashi said. "No ninjutsu, no chakra."

"Well, he's certainly made a fine mess out of you. What a pity."

The comment came from a small man in a black suit. He held a cane in his hands, and his left arm was wrapped in a cast. He wore dark sunglasses, and wiry waves of gray hair grew from the top of his head. Behind him was a small army of scruffy-looking brutes. Each one carried a weapon.

"Hello, Zabuza," Gato said.

"Gato!" Zabuza cried out. "What are you doing here? And why did you bring all of them?"

"Heh heh. There's been a slight change of

plans," Gato explained. "This was what I had in mind all along. I never intended to pay you. I could have hired a skilled ninja from one of the top villages, but they're all too expensive. It's much simpler to hire renegades like yourself. No one cares what I do to your kind once the job is done."

Zabuza grunted. The big warrior looked helpless and defeated.

Gato chuckled, and the mob behind him began to shout.

"You're in no shape to fight us! We can take you down without even breaking a sweat!" one man called out.

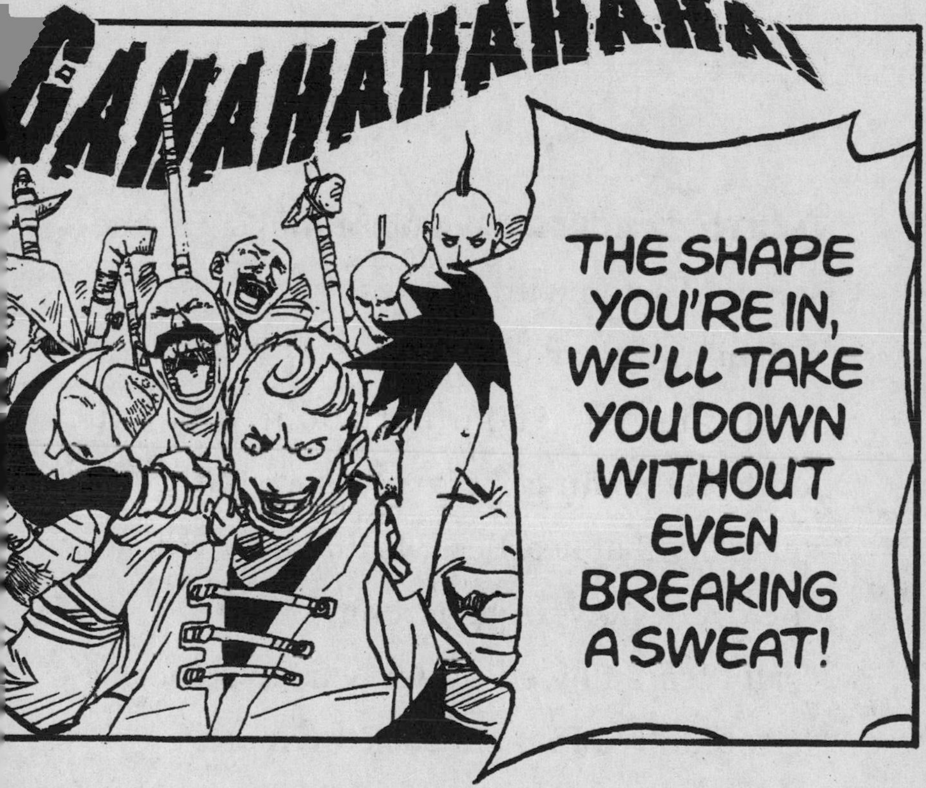
GAHAHAHAHAHAHA!
THE SHAPE YOU'RE IN, WE'LL TAKE YOU DOWN WITHOUT EVEN BREAKING A SWEAT!

NARUTO IGNORED the mob of thugs. He had
a score to settle with Zabuza first.

"Haku did everything for you. But you
don't care how Haku felt about you. You
don't feel a thing!" Naruto shouted. "Are
you really that heartless? Is that how you get
when your powers get strong?"

Hot tears flowed down Naruto's cheeks.
He couldn't hold them back anymore.

"Kid," Zabuza said. "*NOT ANOTHER WORD.*"

Zabuza turned to him, and Naruto saw

that he was crying too.

"It broke his heart to have to fight you and your friends," Zabuza said. "That's the truth. He was too kind, too gentle."

Zabuza used his teeth to rip off the cloth mask that covered the bottom of his face. He spit the cloth aside.

"You're right, you know," he said softly. "Say what we will, do what we will, in the end, we ninja are still people after all. We have feelings. We're **HUMAN**. And I've lost everything."

Naruto looked at Zabuza's face. There was no monster hidden behind that mask. He was definitely human—and sad.

"Would you lend me your kunai?" Zabuza asked.

Naruto would never lend a weapon to an enemy. But Zabuza wasn't his enemy anymore.

"Sure," Naruto replied. He tossed the kunai, and Zabuza caught it between his teeth.

Then he faced Gato and the mob.

Gato was confused. "What?"

Zabuza hurled his body forward, his eyes blazing.

"What are you waiting for? Destroy all of them!" Gato ordered his henchmen.

The men all cheered.

"You may be a ninja, but you don't stand a chance against us!"

Zabuza charged at them. A fiery red light glowed from his body. The light took the shape of a fierce face with horns and fangs.

"A monster!" Gato cried. He hid behind his hired thugs.

Zabuza tore through the mob of people. With the kunai in his mouth, he knocked down man after man. They attacked him with swords and spears, but Zabuza would not fall. Finally he stood facing Gato. He knew this was it for them both.

The memory of Haku came into Zabuza's mind.

"It's goodbye now, Haku," Zabuza said softly. "Thanks for everything. And... I'm sorry."

SASUKE FELT strange. Everything was dark.

Am I still alive? he wondered.

Then he heard Sakura's sobs. Her body shook as she cried on top of him.

"Sakura, your arm's heavy," Sasuke said weakly.

Tazuna gasped. Sakura sat up, shocked. Sasuke opened his eyes.

"SASUKE! SASUKE! SASUKE!" Sakura shrieked. She started to cry again, this time with happiness. She hugged Sasuke tightly.

Sasuke groaned. "Sakura, you're hurting me."

Sakura quickly let go. Sasuke's face was pale and marked with cuts from his battle with Haku.

"I'm okay," he said. "How is Naruto? And that little creep with the mask—what happened to him?"

Sasuke strained to sit up as he talked.

"Don't try to move!" Sakura cried in alarm. "Naruto is fine. But the boy died trying to protect Zabuza. And Zabuza too, after he attacked Gato. They're both gone now."

"Hmm," Sasuke said thoughtfully. "I was afraid. I thought..."

"You're amazing, Sasuke!" Sakura said warmly. "You survived!"

Sasuke lowered his eyes. "No," he said, remembering. *It was the boy. He never planned to kill me from the start.*

Sakura jumped to her feet. "Naruto! It's Sasuke! He's alive!" she called out.

Naruto turned around. He couldn't believe it. Sasuke was standing up. He slowly raised his arm to greet Naruto.

Naruto remembered what Zabuza had said about Haku.

It broke his heart to have to fight you and your friends. He was too kind, too gentle.

Naruto smiled. *I get it.*

Kakashi turned to see Sasuke standing there. "Sasuke made it! Fantastic."

One of the thugs in the mob pounded the bridge with a stick. "Aren't you sweethearts forgetting something?" he shouted.

The henchmen called out threats.

"This is all your fault! We won't get paid now!"

"The only way we can break even is to raid the village!"

"Let's go!"

They waved their weapons and charged down the bridge.

"This isn't good," Kakashi said.

"STOP RIGHT THERE!"

Naruto turned to see a crowd of villagers run onto the bridge—led by Inari! The villagers all held spears and axes.

"This island is our home!" one of the villagers called out. "One step further and you'll never take another step!"

Gato's hired men skidded to a stop.

Tazuna couldn't believe his eyes. "Inari?"

"Inari!" Naruto cheered.

Inari grinned. "Hey! It's about being a hero, you know? All that nick of time stuff."

"Good one, kid," Naruto said. "Mind if I join you? ART OF THE SHADOW DOPPELGANGER!"

The air sizzled with chakra as a dozen copies of Naruto appeared out of thin air behind him. The mob took a step backward.

I can't manage anything solid with my chakra so low, Kakashi thought. *But a bluff should be enough for these bozos.*

"ART OF THE SHADOW DOPPELGANGER—*KAKASHI STYLE!*" Kakashi shouted.

The mob screamed in fear as what looked like a hundred Kakashis appeared on the bridge.

The real Kakashi raised an eyebrow. "Now—shall we?"

"*NEVER MIND!*" yelled one of the henchmen.

"Run away! Run away!" the others cried.

The hired thugs jumped off of the bridge. They splashed into the water and swam away.

The villagers erupted in a loud cheer.

"Hooray!"

"*WE DID IT!*"

INARI!!
HEH HEH.
IT'S BEING A HERO, YOU KNOW? ALL THAT NICK OF TIME STUFF!

TWO WEEKS later, Naruto, Sakura, Sasuke, and Kakashi visited the shady grove where Zabuza and Haku were buried. A wooden cross marked each gravesite. Plates of offerings, like cakes and flowers, sat on the grass in front of each one. Zabuza's sword was stuck into the ground behind his grave.

Hungry, Naruto reached for a cake. Sakura slapped his hand away.

"What are you doing?" Sakura scolded. "Those are not for you!"

Naruto put back the cake. Sakura calmed down.

"Master Kakashi," she began. "I still can't help wondering about those two. Were they right about what a ninja should be?"

"A true ninja is a tool, to serve the land we come from," Kakashi said. "That's as true for us in Leaf Village as it is anywhere else."

Naruto frowned. "Is that really what becoming a full-fledged ninja is about? 'Cause I don't like the sound of it."

"Do you really feel that way, Master Kakashi?" Sasuke asked.

"Well...no," Kakashi admitted. "That's why we ninja live our lives with our ideals bubbling just beneath the surface."

Naruto stared at the two graves.

"That's it. I've made up my mind," he announced. "I'm going to create my own **NINDO**—my own ninja path. My *own* destiny."

DO YOU REALLY FEEL THAT WAY, MASTER KAKASHI?

Kakashi started to correct him, then stopped. He smiled.

The way of Naruto might not be such a bad way after all.

They walked from the graves to the bridge. The villagers had worked hard during the last weeks. It was finally finished. Now the Land of Waves was connected to the rest of the world. They could grow and prosper once more.

Tazuna waited on the bridge with some

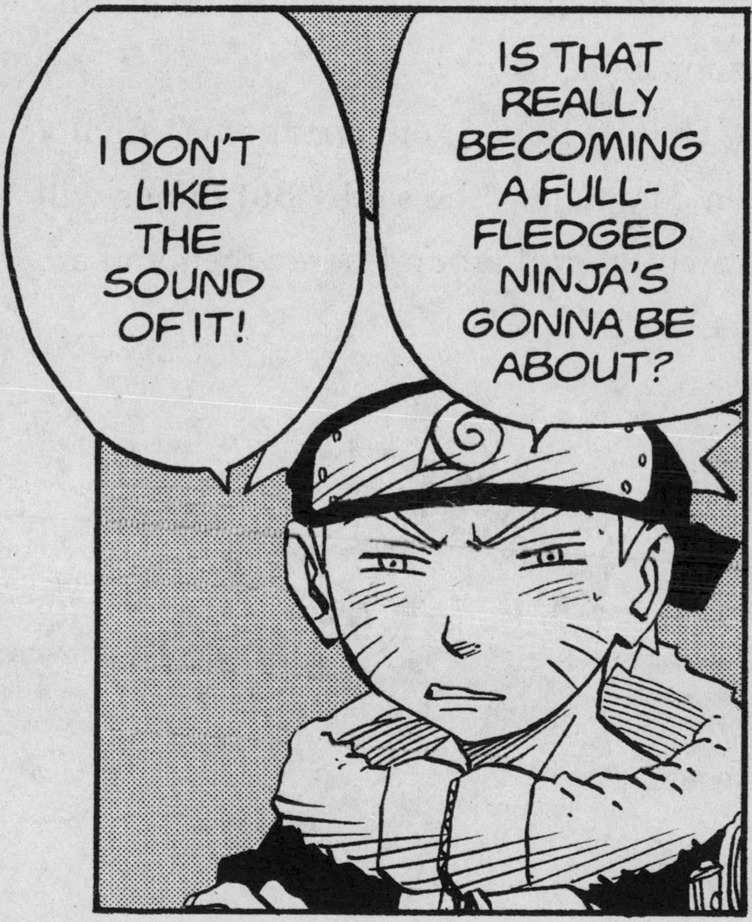
IS THAT REALLY BECOMING A FULL-FLEDGED NINJA'S GONNA BE ABOUT?
I DON'T LIKE THE SOUND OF IT!

of the villagers. His daughter Tsunami and grandson Inari stood on either side of him. Tazuna looked sad.

"Thanks to you, our bridge has finally been completed," he said. "But things will be awfully dull around here when you are gone."

"No problemo, Tazuna, my man! We'll come back to play with you sometime!" Naruto promised.

Little Inari's eyes filled with tears. "You better," he said. His grandfather patted him on the head.

Now Naruto felt like crying too.

"Uh, so, um," he stammered. "Inari, don't let it get you down! It's okay to cry if you want."

"I'm not gonna cry!" Inari shouted. He closed his eyes, holding back the tears. "But Naruto, big brother, you can cry. Go ahead!"

Naruto turned away from him. "Me? No way!" But it was too late. He was already bawling. "See you later."

When Inari saw his hero cry, he joined in.

Then Naruto began to blubber big time. He didn't care who saw him!

Sakura rolled her eyes. "Oh brother!"

Squad Seven walked down the bridge toward the long road home to Leaf Village.

Overhead, gulls swooped and flew on the winds. The sun shone brightly in the deep blue sky.

"When we get home, Master Iruka's gonna take me out to celebrate a mission accomplished!" Naruto bragged.

"Uh, okay," Sakura said. "By the way, Sasuke, when we get home, would you like to go out with me sometime?"

"Uh, no thanks," Sasuke replied.

"No?" Sakura said.

"Hey, I'll go out with you," Naruto said.

"Naruto, knock it off!" Sakura yelled. Tazuna watched them until Naruto's orange jacket was only a speck in the distance.

"That boy touched little Inari's heart, and Inari then touched all the hearts of the people in our city," Tazuna remarked. "Naruto built a bridge that carried us all to hope and courage. And speaking of bridges, we still have to dedicate this one. And there's only one name that will truly fit."

"What are you going to call it?" Tsunami asked.

Tazuna grinned. "How about—**THE GREAT NARUTO BRIDGE?**"

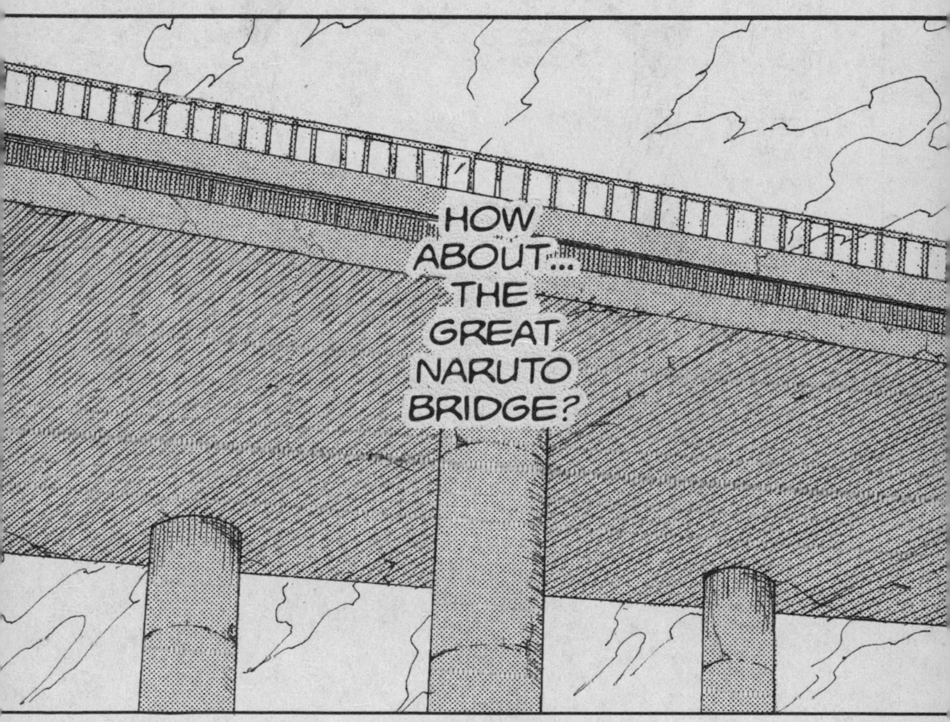
HOW ABOUT... THE GREAT NARUTO BRIDGE?

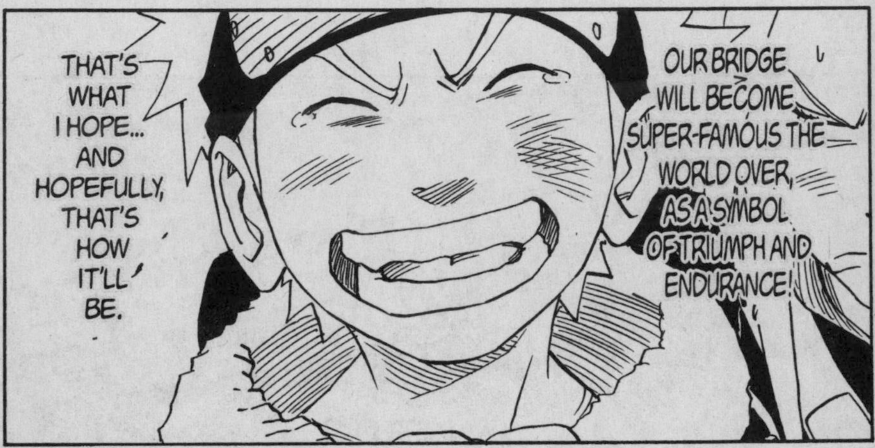
OUR BRIDGE WILL BECOME SUPER-FAMOUS THE WORLD OVER, AS A SYMBOL OF TRIUMPH AND ENDURANCE!
THAT'S WHAT I HOPE... AND HOPEFULLY, THAT'S HOW IT'LL BE.

Ninja Terms

Nindo

A shinobi's *ninja way*, a moral code a ninja follows to stay on the path of good.

Jutsu

Jutsu means "arts" or "techniques." Sometimes referred to as *ninjutsu*, which means more specifically the jutsu of a ninja.

Bunshin

Translated as "doppelganger," this is the art of creating multiple versions of yourself.

Sensei

Teacher

Shuriken

A ninja weapon, a throwing star

Kekkei Genkai

An inherited jutsu that runs in the family.

About the Authors

Author/artist **Masashi Kishimoto** was born in 1974 in rural Okayama Prefecture, Japan. After spending time in art college, he won the Hop Step Award for new manga artists with his manga *Karakuri* (Mechanism). Kishimoto decided to base his next story on traditional Japanese culture. His first version of *Naruto*, drawn in 1997, was a one-shot story about fox spirits; his final version, which debuted in *Weekly Shonen Jump* in 1999, quickly became the most popular ninja manga in Japan. This book is based on that manga.

· · · · · ·

Tracey West is the author of more than 150 books for children and young adults, including the *Pixie Tricks* and *Scream Shop* series. An avid fan of cartoons, comic books, and manga, she has appeared on the New York Times Best Seller List as the author of the Pokémon chapter book adaptations. She currently lives with her family in New York State's Hudson Valley.

The Story of Naruto continues in:
Chapter Book 8
Intruders

Blech! After all their adventures, the time has come for Naruto and his friends Sakura and Sasuke to settle back into their most difficult challenge yet…school! As the three prepare for their new exams, the competition intrudes on their success. Can they prove to their teachers they are still the most powerful ninja kids in all the lands?

BASED ON THE ORIGINAL STORY BY *MASASHI KISHIMOTO*

Adapted by Tracey West

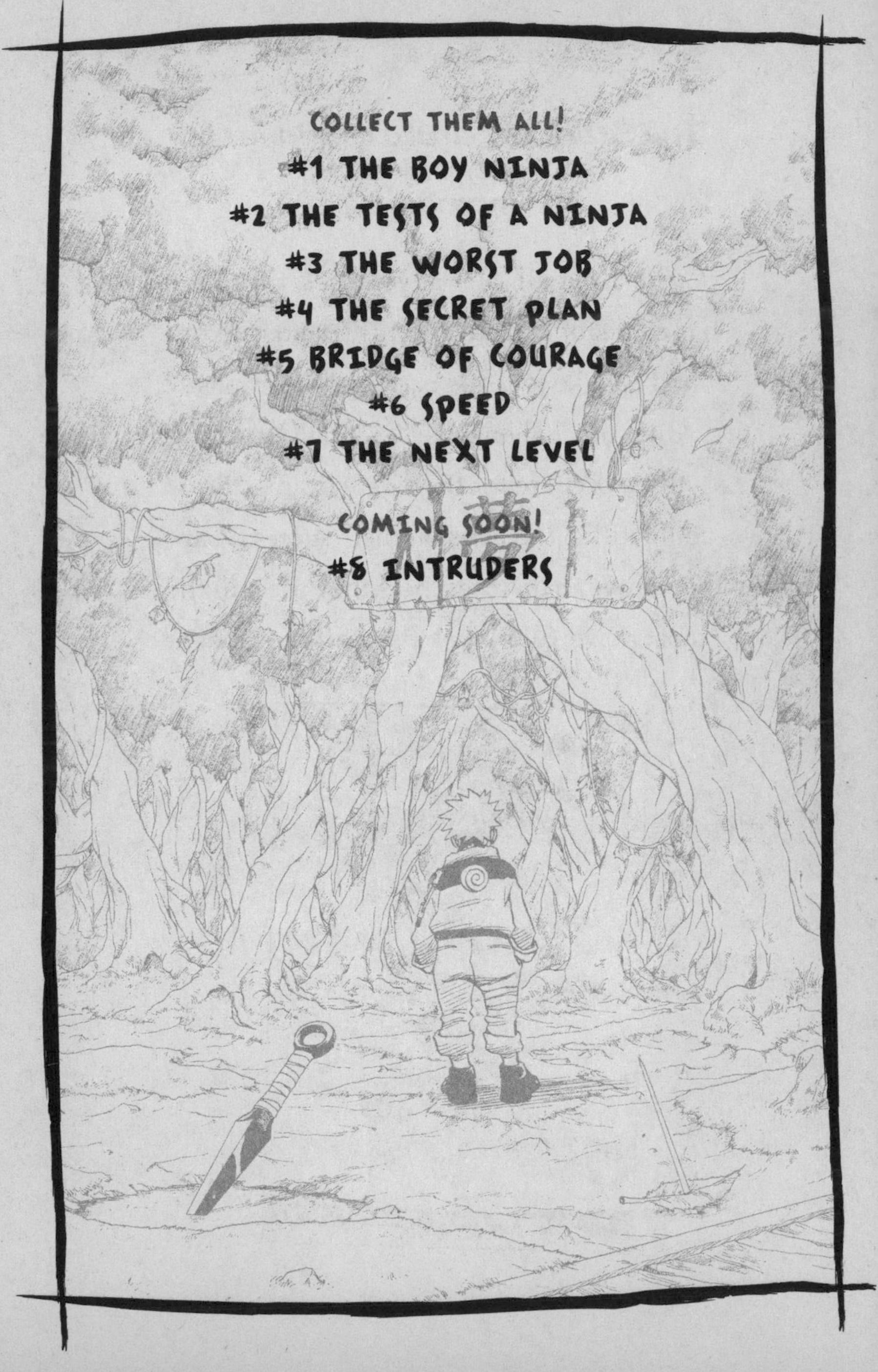

COLLECT THEM ALL!

#1 THE BOY NINJA

#2 THE TESTS OF A NINJA

#3 THE WORST JOB

#4 THE SECRET PLAN

#5 BRIDGE OF COURAGE

#6 SPEED

#7 THE NEXT LEVEL

COMING SOON!

#8 INTRUDERS